W9-AMW-337

# Magic Tree House® Merlin Missions

# MAGIC TREE HOUSE®
## MERLIN MISSIONS

### #1 CHRISTMAS IN CAMELOT

## BY MARY POPE OSBORNE
### ILLUSTRATED BY SAL MURDOCCA

SCHOLASTIC INC.

*For Mallory Loehr,*

*the <u>real</u> Keeper of the Cauldron*

Originally published as Magic Tree House #29 by Random House Children's Books, New York, in 2001.

ISBN 978-1-338-22453-5

12 11 10 9 8 7 6 5 4 3 2          17 18 19 20 21 22

Printed in the U.S.A.                                    40

This edition first printing, September 2017

# CONTENTS

# CONTENTS

*O brother, had you known our Camelot,*
*Built by old kings, age after age, so old*
*The King himself had fears that it would fall,*
*So strange, and rich, and dim . . .*

Alfred Lord Tennyson
*Idylls of the King*

# Prologue

*O*nce upon a time, in Frog Creek, Pennsylvania, a mysterious tree house appeared in the woods. A boy named Jack and his sister, Annie, climbed into the tree house. They found that it was filled with books.

Jack and Annie soon discovered that the tree house was magic. It could take them to the places they read about in the books. All they had to do was point to a picture and wish to go there. They discovered that during their adventures, no time at all passed in Frog Creek.

*Jack and Annie eventually learned that the tree house belonged to Morgan le Fay, an enchantress from Camelot, the long-ago kingdom of King Arthur. On one of their journeys, Jack and Annie visited Morgan's library in Camelot and brought hope and courage to King Arthur.*

*Now it is winter. Jack and Annie have not seen Morgan or the magic tree house for many months. . . .*

## CHAPTER ONE

# A Royal Invitation

Sunlight had faded from the late-afternoon sky. Puffy snow clouds were moving in.

"Let's hurry. I'm cold," said Jack.

He and Annie were walking home from school. Their Christmas vacation was just beginning.

*Cooo—cooo.*

"Wait," said Annie. "Look."

She pointed to a white bird sitting on a bare tree branch at the edge of the woods. The bird was staring straight at them.

"It's a dove," said Jack.

"It's a messenger," said Annie, "from Morgan."

"No," Jack said, afraid to get his hopes up. They hadn't seen Morgan le Fay in a long time. He really missed her.

"*Yes,*" said Annie. "She has a mission for us. I can feel it."

In the hush of the cold twilight, the dove spread its wings and flew into the Frog Creek woods.

"Come on!" said Annie. "The tree house is back!"

"You're just hoping!" said Jack.

"I'm *knowing!*" said Annie. She ran into the woods, following the white dove.

"Oh, brother," said Jack. But he took off after Annie.

Even in the growing darkness, they easily found their way. They zigzagged between the bare trees and ran over the frozen ground until they came to the tallest oak in the woods.

"See?" said Annie, pointing to the top of the tree.

"Yeah," whispered Jack.

There it was: the magic tree house.

"Morgan!" shouted Annie.

Jack held his breath, waiting to see the enchantress at the tree house window. But Morgan did not appear.

Annie grabbed the rope ladder and started up. Jack followed.

When they climbed inside the tree house, Jack saw something lying on the floor. It was a scroll, rolled up and tied with a red velvet ribbon.

Jack picked up the scroll and unrolled it. The thick, yellowed paper shimmered with large gold writing.

"Wow, Morgan sent us a really fancy note," said Annie.

"It's an invitation," said Jack. "Listen."

Dear Jack and Annie,
Please accept this Royal
Invitation to spend Christmas
in the Kingdom of Camelot.
—M.

*"Christmas in Camelot!"* said Annie. "I don't believe it!"

"Cool," whispered Jack. He pictured a beautiful, glowing castle lit with candles and filled with knights and ladies feasting and singing.

"We're going to celebrate Christmas with Morgan and King Arthur!" said Annie. "And Queen Guinevere!"

"Yeah," said Jack. "And the Knights of the Round Table, like Sir Lancelot!"

"Let's go!" said Annie. "Where's the book?"

She and Jack looked around the tree house for a book about Camelot. The only book they saw was the Pennsylvania book that always brought them home.

"That's strange," said Jack. "Morgan didn't send a book about Camelot with the Royal Invitation. How does she expect us to get there?"

"I don't know," said Annie. "Maybe she forgot."

Jack picked up the invitation. He read it again. He turned it over, hoping to find more information. The back of the scroll was blank. He handed the invitation to Annie.

"She must have forgotten," he said.

"Darn," said Annie, staring at the gold writing. "I really wish we could go to Camelot."

The tree branches rustled.

The wind began to blow.

"What's happening?" said Jack.

"I don't know—" said Annie.

"Wait a minute," said Jack. "You were hold-ing the invitation, and you made a wish. . . ."

The wind blew harder.

"That must have made the magic work!" cried Annie.

Jack felt a surge of joy.

"We're going to Camelot!" he said.

The tree house started to spin.

It spun faster and faster.

Then everything was still.

Absolutely still.

# CHAPTER TWO

## This Is Camelot?

Jack shivered. He could see his breath in the dim light.

Annie was staring out the window. "*This* is Camelot?" she said.

Jack looked out with her. The tree house had landed in a grove of tall, bare trees. A huge, dark castle loomed against the gray sky. No light shone from its windows. No banners waved from its turrets. Wind whistled through its tall towers, sounding sad and lonely.

"It looks deserted," said Annie.

"Yeah," said Jack. "I hope we came to the right place."

Jack pulled his notebook and pencil out of his pack. He wanted to write a description of the dark castle.

"Hey, I see someone," said Annie.

Jack looked out the window again.

A woman was crossing the castle draw-bridge. She wore a long cloak and carried a lantern. Her white hair blew in the wind.

"Morgan!" said Annie and Jack together. They laughed with relief.

Morgan hurried over the frost-covered ground toward the grove of trees. "Annie? Jack? Is that you?" she called.

"Of course! Who'd you think?" shouted Annie. She started down from the tree house.

Jack threw his notebook into his backpack. He followed Annie down the rope ladder. When they reached the icy ground, they ran to Morgan and both threw their arms around her.

"I was looking out a window in the castle and saw a bright flash in the orchard," said Morgan. "What are you doing here?"

"You didn't send the tree house for us?" asked Jack.

"With a Royal Invitation to spend Christmas in Camelot?" asked Annie.

"No!" said Morgan. She sounded alarmed.

"But the invitation was signed with an *M*," said Jack.

"I don't understand . . . ," said Morgan. "We are not celebrating Christmas in Camelot this year."

"You aren't?" said Jack.

"Why not?" said Annie.

A look of sadness crossed Morgan's face. "Do you remember when you visited my library and gave King Arthur the hope and courage to challenge his enemy?" she asked.

"Sure," said Jack.

"Well, Arthur's enemy was a man named Mordred," said Morgan. "After you left, Arthur defeated him, but not before Mordred's Dark Wizard cast a spell over the whole kingdom. The spell robbed Camelot of all its joy."

"What? All its *joy*?" whispered Annie.

"Yes," said Morgan. "For months, Camelot has been without music, without celebration, and without laughter."

"Oh, no," said Annie.

"What can we do to help?" said Jack.

Morgan smiled sadly. "This time, I don't think you can do anything," she said. "But perhaps it will lift Arthur's spirits to see you both again. Come, let us go inside the castle."

Morgan held up her lantern and started toward the drawbridge.

Jack and Annie hurried after her. As they walked through the outer courtyard, the frozen grass cracked under their sneakers.

They followed Morgan over the bridge and through a tall gate. There were no signs of life in the castle's inner courtyard.

"Where is everyone?" Annie whispered to Jack.

"I don't know," he whispered back. Jack really wished they had a book about Camelot. It might help them understand what was going on.

Morgan led them to a huge archway with two wooden doors. She stopped and looked at them.

"I am afraid *no* book would help you tonight, Jack," she said.

Jack was startled that Morgan had read his thoughts.

"Why not?" asked Annie.

"On all your other journeys, you visited *real* places and times in history," said Morgan. "Camelot is different."

"How?" said Jack.

"The story of Camelot is a legend," said Morgan. "A legend is a story that begins in truth. But then imagination takes over. Different people in different times tell the story. They use their imaginations to add new parts. That is how a legend is kept alive."

"Tonight we'll add *our* part," said Annie.

"Yes," said Morgan. "And please, I beg you"—in the lantern light, she looked very serious—"do not let the story of Camelot end forever. Keep our kingdom alive."

"Of course we will!" said Annie.

"Good," said Morgan. "Come, then. Let us go into the great hall and see the king."

Morgan lifted an iron latch and pushed open the heavy doors. Jack and Annie followed her into the dark castle.

# CHAPTER THREE

# The Knights of the Round Table

A pair of torches dimly lit the drafty entrance hall of the castle. Shadows danced on the worn tapestries.

"Wait here," said Morgan. "I will tell the king of your arrival." She headed through the huge stone archway that led to the great hall.

"Let's peek in," Annie said to Jack.

Jack pushed his glasses into place. He and Annie walked quietly over to the big arch and peered in.

The ceiling of the great hall towered high

above a stone floor. At the far end of the room,
King Arthur and his knights were sitting
around a huge, round table. They all wore
brown tunics. They had shaggy hair and beards.

Their names were carved in gold letters on the backs of their chairs.

"The Knights of the Round Table!" whispered Jack.

Morgan was talking to King Arthur. Beside the king sat a woman in a plain gray robe. She had pale skin and brown, curly hair.

"Queen Guinevere," whispered Annie.

Morgan left the king, and Jack and Annie moved quickly back into the shadows. A moment later, Morgan appeared.

"I told the king that two special friends of his have just arrived," she said. "Come with me."

As they walked with Morgan through the great hall, Jack shivered. The huge room was drafty and damp. There was no fire in the fireplace. The stone floor was so cold that Jack could feel the chill through his sneakers.

They stopped near the Round Table. King Arthur stared at them with his piercing gray eyes.

"Greetings from Frog Creek," Annie said to the king and queen. Annie bowed, and Jack bowed, too.

The queen smiled. But King Arthur did not.

"Your Majesty, you remember Jack and Annie?" said Morgan. "You met them last summer in my library?"

"Indeed, I shall never forget them," King Arthur said softly. "Greetings, Annie. Greetings, Jack. How do you come to be in Camelot on this bleak night?"

"We came in the magic tree house," said Annie.

A shadow crossed the king's face. He looked at Morgan.

"No, Your Majesty. I did not use my magic to bring them here," she said. "Perhaps a bit of magic still lingers in the tree house, and it traveled on its own."

*What's going on?* Jack wondered. *Why does King Arthur seem unhappy about the magic tree house?*

King Arthur looked back at Jack and Annie.

"However you have come, you are welcome in my kingdom," he said. He turned to the queen. "Guinevere, these are the two friends who once gave me hope and courage in a time of need."

Queen Guinevere smiled again. But there was a sad look in her eyes. "I have heard much about you," she said.

"I've heard about you, too!" said Annie.

"Allow me to present my knights," said King Arthur. "Sir Bors, Sir Kay, Sir Tristram . . ."

As the king named each knight, Jack and Annie nodded shyly. The knights nodded at them in return. Jack waited to hear the name *Sir Lancelot*, the most famous of Camelot's knights. But the king never said it.

"And finally, Sir Bedivere and Sir Gawain," King Arthur said.

The king then turned to three empty chairs at the table. "And there once sat three who are lost to us now," he said.

*Lost how?* wondered Jack.

"You may sit at their places and join our dinner," King Arthur said.

"Thank you," said Annie.

Following Morgan around the table, Jack read the names carved on the backs of the three empty chairs: SIR LANCELOT, SIR GALAHAD, SIR PERCIVAL.

Jack took off his backpack and sat down in Sir Lancelot's place.

As he sat tall and straight in the heavy wooden chair, Jack looked at the king and his knights. They were gnawing meat off bones and slurping wine from heavy goblets. They ate without manners or delight.

Jack really wanted to take notes. He reached into his pack under the table and pulled out his notebook and pencil. But before he could write a word, a serving boy brought more food. Jack quickly put his things away. The boy set a greasy slab of beef on a soggy piece of bread in front of him. The food looked terrible.

"Not much of a Christmas feast, huh?" Annie said in a low voice.

Jack shook his head.

Annie leaned close to Morgan and whispered so King Arthur wouldn't hear. "What happened to the three lost knights?" she asked.

"After Mordred's Dark Wizard cast his spell, the king sought help from the magicians of Camelot," Morgan said quietly. "They told him he must send his knights on a quest to the Otherworld, to recapture our kingdom's joy."

"What's the Otherworld?" said Jack.

"It is an ancient, enchanted land beyond the edge of the Earth," said Morgan. "The place where all magic first began."

"Wow," whispered Annie.

"The king chose his three bravest knights to journey there," said Morgan. "When they did not come back, Arthur turned against his magicians. He blamed magic for all of Camelot's woes. Hence, he has banned magic of any kind from the kingdom forever."

"But *you're* a magician," whispered Annie. "Did the king turn against you, too?"

"Arthur and I have a long friendship," said Morgan. "He has allowed me to stay in the castle as long as I promise not to practice the art of magic ever again."

A feeling of dread crept over Jack. "So . . . does that mean the magic tree house is . . . ?"

Morgan nodded. "Yes. Banished from Camelot," she said. "I'm afraid this will be your last journey. And the last time we see each other." Her eyes filled with tears. She looked away.

"What? The last time we see each other? *Forever?*" said Annie.

Before Morgan could answer, the wooden doors swung open with a bang. A wind rushed through the great hall. The torches and candles flamed brighter, making the shadows leap wildly on the walls.

The sound of hoofbeats filled the room. A knight on a huge horse rode through the arched doorway.

The knight was dressed all in red—from his shining helmet to the long cloak on his back. His horse was dressed all in green—from the armor that covered his head to the cloth that hung from his saddle.

"Oh, wow!" breathed Annie. "A Christmas Knight!"

## CHAPTER FOUR

# Who Will Go?

"I have come to see Arthur the king!" the Christmas Knight said. His deep voice echoed from inside his helmet. His red armor gleamed in the firelight.

King Arthur stood up. He stared fiercely at the knight, but he spoke in a calm, steady voice. "*I* am Arthur the king," he said. "Who are you?"

The knight did not answer Arthur's question. "So. You are the legendary King Arthur of Camelot," he said in a mocking voice. "And these must be the famous Knights of the Round Table."

"Yes," said King Arthur, "and again, I ask: Who are *you*?"

The Christmas Knight still did not answer Arthur's question.

"The spell of the Dark Wizard has robbed Camelot of its joy," said the Christmas Knight. "Has it robbed you and your men of your *courage* as well?"

"You dare to question our courage?" King Arthur said in a low, angry voice.

"CAMELOT IS DYING!" the Christmas Knight boomed. "Why has no one journeyed to the Otherworld to recapture its joy?"

"I have sent my best knights on such a quest," said King Arthur. "They never returned."

"THEN SEND MORE!" thundered the Christmas Knight.

"NO!" shouted King Arthur, pounding his fists on the table. "*Never again* will I feed good men to the magic and monsters of the Other-world!"

Jack felt a chill of fear. *What monsters?*

"Then you choose your fate," said the Christmas Knight. "If you will send no one else to the Otherworld, all that your kingdom has gained through time—all beauty, music, wonder, and light, all that Camelot has ever been or could ever be—will be lost and forgotten forever."

"No!" shouted Annie.

"Shh, Annie!" said Jack.

The Christmas Knight turned to the knights at the table. "WHO WILL GO?" he boomed.

"*We* will!" shouted Annie.

"We will?" said Jack.

"Yes! We'll go on the quest!" Annie yelled. She jumped up.

"No!" cried Morgan le Fay.

"Never!" said King Arthur.

"Annie!" said Jack. He leaped up from his chair and tried to grab her.

"YES!" thundered the Christmas Knight. He pointed his red-gloved hand at Annie and Jack. "The youngest of all—these two—they will go."

"You are mocking us!" King Arthur shouted.

"THEY WILL GO!" boomed the knight. His words echoed throughout the hall.

*Oh, no*, thought Jack.

"Yes!" said Annie. She pulled Jack toward the Christmas Knight.

King Arthur turned to his men. "Stop them!"

Several knights started to rush toward Jack

and Annie. The Christmas Knight raised his gloved hand high in the air.

In an instant, the room fell deathly quiet.

Everyone around the table was as still as a statue.

King Arthur looked like the statue of a furious king. Queen Guinevere looked like the statue of a worried queen. The Knights of the Round Table looked like statues of fierce knights.

And Morgan le Fay looked like the statue of a caring friend. Her mouth was open, as if she were calling out to Jack and Annie. But no sound came from her lips—no sound at all.

## CHAPTER FIVE

# Rhymes of the Christmas Knight

"**M**organ?" said Annie.

Annie ran to the table. She touched Morgan's cheek, then quickly pulled back her hand.

"She's cold. She's as cold as ice!" said Annie. Tears filled her eyes.

Annie turned to the Christmas Knight in a fury. "What did you do to Morgan?" she asked. "Bring her back!"

"Do not fear," said the Christmas Knight. His voice was softer and kinder. "She will come back to life after you complete your quest."

"What—what exactly is our quest?" said Jack.

"You must journey to the Otherworld," said the Christmas Knight. "There you will find a cauldron. The cauldron is filled with the Water of Memory and Imagination. You must bring a cup of the water back to Camelot. If you fail, Camelot will never come back to life. *Never.*"

"How do we do all that?" asked Annie, wiping her eyes.

"Remember these three rhymes," said the Christmas Knight.

"Wait, let me write them down," said Jack.

His hands trembled as he pulled out his notebook and pencil. He looked at the Christmas Knight.

"Okay, I'm ready," he said. Gripping his pencil made Jack feel stronger.

The knight's voice rang out from inside his helmet.

*"Beyond the iron gate*
*The Keepers of the Cauldron wait."*

Jack quickly wrote down the knight's words. "Okay, what's next?" he asked.

The Christmas Knight went on:

*"Four gifts you will need—*
*The first from me.*
*Then a cup, a compass,*
*And, finally, a key."*

"Cup . . . compass . . . key. . . . Got it," said Jack.

The Christmas Knight's voice boomed again:

*"If you survive to complete your quest,*
*The secret door lies to the west."*

Jack copied down the last rhyme, then looked up at the knight.

"Anything else?" he asked.

Without a word, the knight pulled off his red cloak. He dropped it to the floor. It fell silently into a heap at Jack and Annie's feet.

The Christmas Knight snapped his horse's red reins, then galloped out of the great hall.

## CHAPTER SIX

## A White Comet

Once the knight was gone, the candles and torches in the great hall grew dimmer. A bitter chill crept over the room.

"What do these three rhymes mean?" said Jack, looking at his notebook. "Who are the Keepers of the Cauldron? What secret door?"

"I don't know," said Annie. "I just know we have to save Morgan."

She gathered the red cloak up in her arms. "We've got our first gift," she said. "Let's go."

"Wait—we should figure this out first," said Jack.

"No. We should just go," said Annie. She turned and headed for the archway.

Jack pushed his glasses into place and looked back at the Round Table, at the frozen king and queen, at the frozen knights, and at Morgan le Fay.

He loved Morgan. She was their great friend and teacher. If he and Annie did not go on their quest, Morgan's story and the stories of Camelot and all the stories about the magic tree house would end forever.

Jack took a deep breath. He put his notebook into his backpack. Then he turned toward the archway.

"Annie?" he said.

She was gone.

"Annie, wait!" he shouted. "Wait!"

Jack ran out of the great hall.

"Annie!"

"I'm here," she said quietly. "I'm waiting." She was standing at the end of the entrance hall peering outside.

"How do we get to the Otherworld?" she asked.

"Maybe the tree house can take us there," said Jack. "Come on."

Together, Jack and Annie hurried through the inner courtyard of the castle and over the drawbridge. They ran over the frozen ground to the moonlit grove of trees.

Clutching the red cloak, Annie started up the rope ladder. Jack followed. They climbed inside the tree house and sat on the floor.

Annie picked up the Royal Invitation. "Close your eyes. I'll make the wish," she said.

Jack closed his eyes. He was shivering from the cold.

"I wish we could go to the Otherworld," said Annie.

The bare branches of the trees rattled in the wind.

"I think it's working!" whispered Annie.

The wind stopped blowing.

Jack opened his eyes. He and Annie looked out the window. The dark castle loomed against the sky. They were still in Camelot.

"It d-didn't work," said Jack, his teeth chattering.

"Yes, it did!" whispered Annie. "Look down."

Standing below the tree house was the biggest deer Jack had ever seen. The deer was staring up at them with amber eyes. His huge antlers seemed to glow in the cold moonlight.

Most amazing of all, the deer was completely white, as white as new-fallen snow.

"A white stag!" said Jack.

Puffs of frosty air blew from the stag's nostrils. He stepped toward the tree house and shook his giant head.

"He's come to take us on our journey," said Annie.

"People don't ride deer," said Jack.

But Annie had already started down the rope ladder. Jack watched from the window as she walked to the stag and spoke softly. The stag knelt. Annie climbed on his back.

"Come on!" she called to Jack. "Bring the cloak!"

"Okay, okay," said Jack. He gathered up the heavy velvet cloak. Clutching it against his chest, he climbed down the rope ladder. He hurried over to Annie and the white stag.

"Put on the cloak and climb on behind me," said Annie.

Jack put the cloak on over his backpack. He pulled it around his shoulders and buttoned it at the neck. As the cloak fell down around his body, the soft, smooth cloth made him feel warm and safe.

"Ready?" said Annie.

"Yeah," said Jack. He climbed on the stag's back behind Annie.

The white stag slowly stood up. Annie leaned forward, putting her arms around its neck. Jack leaned forward, too, and held on to Annie. The

red velvet cloak draped over both of them, falling past their feet.

The white stag stepped gracefully over the frozen grass. He walked through the outer gate of the castle. He blew out a puff of air, then broke into a leaping run.

Jack held on tightly to Annie as the stag dashed across a frost-covered field. He jumped over hedgerows and stone walls. He bounded across icy streams.

Annie's braids floated on the wind. The red cloak billowed behind them. Jack was amazed at how easy it was to ride on the stag's back. He felt calm and safe as the stag sped like a white comet through the wintry countryside.

The stag ran past flocks of sheep and herds of goats asleep in the meadows. He ran past thatched huts and quiet stables.

The stag ran on and on through the starry night. Jack saw a cloud-covered mountain range in the distance. When they came close to the craggy mountains, Jack was sure the stag would stop. But he galloped on—not even breaking his stride as he started up a rocky slope.

The stag finally came to a halt on the ledge of a steep cliff. In a windy swirl of fog and cloud, he knelt to the ground, and Jack and Annie slid off his back.

The stag stood up. He stared down at them with his glowing amber eyes.

"Thank you!" said Annie. "Do you have to leave now?"

The stag lowered his head and raised it again. He blew out a frosty puff of air, then leaped away, vanishing into the mist.

"Bye," Annie said wistfully. She stared into the mist for a moment, then turned to Jack. "What do we do now?"

"I don't know," said Jack. "Let's read the three rhymes again."

He reached under the red cloak and pulled off his pack. He took out his notebook and started to read the first rhyme:

*"Beyond the iron gate—"*

"Jack!" interrupted Annie. "Look!"

Jack looked up. The wind had blown away some of the fog. Beyond the cliff rose another mountain. A huge gate was built into its side. A pale light shone between the gate's thick iron bars. Two knights in gold armor stood guard under flaming torches.

"Oh, man," whispered Jack.

"That's it—the iron gate!" said Annie. "If we pass through that gate, we'll be in the Otherworld!"

# CHAPTER SEVEN

## A Good Trick

As the wind blew away more fog, Jack and Annie saw a bridge. It was made of thick wooden planks held together with iron bands. It stretched all the way from the edge of the cliff where they were standing to the iron gate.

"Come on, let's go!" said Annie.

"Wait!" said Jack. "What about the guards?"

The two guards in gold armor stood perfectly still. Their huge spears gleamed in the torch-light.

"I don't know," said Annie. "Read the second rhyme."

Jack looked in his notebook and read aloud.

"*Four gifts you will need—*
*The first from me.*
*Then a cup, a compass,*
*And, finally, a key.*"

"The first gift is the Christmas Knight's cloak," said Annie.

"Yeah, I guess it's supposed to help us somehow," said Jack.

He unbuttoned the cloak from around his neck. Then he held it out to get a good look at it.

"Maybe it can make us invisible," said Annie.

"That's nuts," said Jack.

"Seriously," she said, "cloaks sometimes do that in stories."

"Well, it didn't make *me* invisible, did it?" said Jack.

"Maybe you were wearing it wrong," said Annie. "Give it to me."

"Oh, brother," said Jack. But he handed the cloak to Annie. It flapped in the wind as she pulled it around her shoulders.

"Can you see me?" she said.

"Yes, Annie," said Jack, rolling his eyes. "I can see you."

Jack looked back at the gate. *Even if we get past the guards, what then?* he wondered. *The Otherworld swallowed up Camelot's best knights. King Arthur said it was filled with magic and monsters.*

"Jack! Look at me now."

Jack turned to Annie. She wasn't there.

"Where are you?" he said, staring at the darkness.

"Cool, it works!"

"Where are you?" Jack said again, turning around.

"Here."

Jack felt a hand touch his face.

"Ahh!" he said, jumping back.

"It's me! I'm invisible! I pulled the hood over my head. That's the trick."

Jack felt a chill run down his spine.

"Oh, man," he whispered.

"Watch. I'm going to take the hood off."

In a flash, Annie was back.

"It feels creepy to be invisible," she said.

Jack was speechless.

"The magic only happens when you wear the hood," said Annie. "Good trick, huh?"

"Uh—yeah," said Jack. He shook his head. "This is just too weird."

"Don't worry about it being weird. It's a great way to get past the guards," said Annie. "Plus it's a way to hide in the Otherworld. We don't know what we'll find there, right?"

"Yeah, right," said Jack. "Okay."

"Good," said Annie. "Now, stand beside me and don't move."

Jack put away his notebook. Annie threw the velvet cloak over his shoulders and backpack.

"Great. It's big enough for both of us," she said. She carefully arranged the folds around them. Then she pulled the huge hood over both their heads.

Jack looked down. He couldn't see his body at all! He felt like he couldn't breathe. In a panic, he threw off the hood.

"I hate that!" he said.

"I told you it's creepy," said Annie. "But if we don't wear it, we won't get past the guards."

"Yeah, I know, and we won't have protection in the Otherworld," said Jack. He took a deep breath. "Okay. Let's do it."

Annie pulled the hood up again.

"I'll hold on to the hood so it won't blow off," she said. "You just think about getting across that bridge. Nothing else."

"But I can't see my feet," said Jack.

"You don't need to see your feet to walk!" said Annie. "Come on. Do it for Morgan!"

"Right," said Jack.

He and Annie stepped onto the bridge.

"Whatever you do, don't look down," said Annie.

As they started over the bridge, the wind whistled around them. Jack couldn't help it—he looked down.

Not only was his body missing, but the fog beneath the bridge was moving in a wild, spinning whirl. Jack felt dizzy and faint. He stopped.

"Keep going," whispered Annie.

Jack took a deep breath and looked straight ahead. Then he started walking again. He went slowly—step by step—toward the pale light beyond the bars of the gate.

In the flickering torchlight, the guards looked like giants. As Jack and Annie slipped invisibly by them, Jack held his breath.

*How will we open the gate?* he wondered.

"*WHOOOSSSHHH!*" said Annie loudly.

Jack's heart nearly stopped. Had Annie lost her mind? "What are you doing?" he whispered.

"I'm the wind!" Annie whispered back. *"WHOOOSSSHHH!"*

Annie gave the gate a shove. It swung open, as if pushed by the wind.

Jack looked back and saw that the guards had turned in their direction.

"Quick!" whispered Annie.

She and Jack moved silently through the gateway.

*"WHOOOSSSHHH!"* said Annie.

She pushed the gate back. It shut with a *clang*. Through the bars, Jack saw the guards face the bridge again.

"Good work," he said to Annie.

"Thanks," she said.

Jack and Annie then turned away from the gate.

*"Ohh!"* whispered Annie.

*"The Otherworld,"* whispered Jack.

## CHAPTER EIGHT

# The Otherworld

The Otherworld was completely different from the dark, cold world Jack and Annie had just left behind.

They were standing at the edge of a pale green meadow. The meadow was bathed in warm, rosy sunlight. Three horses—one black, one brown, one gray—were grazing nearby. On a hillside beyond the meadow, red and purple flowers sparkled like bright buttons.

"It's so *nice* here," said Annie.

"Yeah," said Jack. "Maybe we won't need *this*

anymore." He pulled the hood of the cloak off their heads. He was relieved to see Annie's face—and to see himself!

"What was the first rhyme again?" asked Annie.

Jack took out his notebook. He found the first rhyme and read aloud:

*"Beyond the iron gate*
*The Keepers of the Cauldron wait."*

He looked around warily. "I wonder where the Keepers of the Cauldron are?" he said.

"What do you mean?" asked Annie. "We just sneaked past them. Remember? WHOOOSH?"

"I don't know," said Jack. "The rhyme says *'beyond* the iron gate.' Those guards were standing *in front of* the gate. They weren't *beyond* it."

"Shh," said Annie. "Listen. . . ."

From over the hill came the faint sounds of sweet, joyful music.

"Maybe the Keepers of the Cauldron are playing that music," said Annie.

"Maybe . . . ," said Jack. He listened for a moment and smiled. The music made him feel light and happy.

"Let's go meet the Keepers!" said Annie.

"Not so fast," said Jack. "Shouldn't we be invisible again? Just in case?"

"I guess so," said Annie, sighing.

Jack pulled the hood of the cloak over their heads. Together, they started walking invisibly across the soft meadow. They passed the three horses and climbed the flower-covered hill. At the top, they looked down.

"Oh, man," said Jack.

The hill sloped gently down into a misty green glade. In the middle of the glade, a band of musicians played flutes and pipes, drums and violins. Around the band, hundreds of dancers danced in a huge circle.

"The Keepers of the Cauldron!" said Annie.

The dancers and musicians were smiling and laughing. They wore blue coats and green coats, white gowns and yellow gowns. They wore sparkling red slippers and hats with colored feathers.

The dancers looked like people—except they all had glittering gold skin and wings that shimmered in the mist like spun silver.

"They're beautiful!" said Annie.

"Yeah, they are," said Jack.

"I don't think we need to be invisible with them," said Annie.

"I think you're right," said Jack.

He and Annie threw off the red cloak. They left it in the dewy grass and ran down the hillside to the winged dancers. The dancers paid no attention to them. They just kept going around and around in their joyous circle.

"I feel like dancing with them!" said Annie.

"Me too!" said Jack. It was strange—he was usually shy about dancing. But he wanted to join this dance more than anything.

Jack pulled off his backpack. As he set it down, he saw three swords lying in the grass.

But he didn't stop to wonder about them. The music was calling.

The winged dancers broke their circle and welcomed Jack and Annie into their dance. Annie held Jack's right hand as he grasped the slender golden hand of the dancer on his left.

The dancer smiled down at him. Like the others, she was as tall as a grownup. But she didn't have any lines or wrinkles on her face. All the dancers looked very young—yet they seemed ancient at the same time.

As Jack danced around in the circle, his heart leaped. His spirits soared. His glasses fell off, but he didn't care. He kept dancing. As he danced, everything in his mind became a blur. He forgot about Morgan and Camelot. He forgot about the quest for the Water of Memory and Imagination. He forgot all his fears and worries.

"Jack, look!" Annie cried.

Jack looked at her. "Hi!" he shouted, laughing.

"No! Don't look at me!" she called. "Look there! Look across the circle!"

"I can't see!" he said.

"Three knights!" Annie shouted. "Three knights dancing!"

"Great!" Jack shouted.

"No, Jack! They look awful! They look sick!" Annie yelled. She pulled away from the circle and tumbled back into the grass.

"Jack!" she called. "Stop dancing!"

But Jack didn't want to stop. He wanted to dance to the wild music forever. Forever . . . and ever . . . and ever.

# CHAPTER NINE

# The Lost Knights

Annie chased Jack around the circle.

"Stop, Jack!" she cried. "Stop!" She grabbed his shirt and tried to pull him out of the dance.

"Let go, Annie!" he said. "Leave me alone!"

But Annie wouldn't let go. Finally, she pulled so hard that Jack broke hands with the dancers and tumbled backward into the grass.

The winged dancers didn't seem to notice. They closed their circle and kept going around and around.

"Why did you do that?" said Jack, sitting up. "I was having fun!"

"Look at the knights!" said Annie. "See them?"

Jack still couldn't see. The world was spinning before his eyes. He ached to get back into the dance.

"Here, I found your glasses!" said Annie. "Put them on!"

Jack put on his glasses. He peered at the circle of dancers. He caught sight of armor glinting in the sunlight. He saw three knights dancing in a row. Two of them looked very young. The third looked much older.

As they came closer, Jack saw their faces. All the joy of the music drained out of him. The knights looked tired and sick. Their hair and beards were long and scraggly. Their faces were bony and pale. Their eyes stared wildly and their lips were frozen in ghostly smiles.

"What's *wrong* with them?" asked Jack.

"They can't stop dancing!" said Annie. "They're dancing themselves to death!"

"They must be the lost knights from Camelot," said Jack.

"We have to save them!" said Annie.

"Yeah," said Jack. He tried to clear his mind and think. "What about this? We get back in the dance—and we take places between the dancers and the knights."

"Yes! Then we can pull the knights out of the circle!" said Annie.

"Wait," said Jack. "What if I can't stop dancing again?"

"Just don't let yourself get caught by the music," said Annie. "You have to think about something else. Think about why we're here. Think about Morgan."

"Okay," said Jack. "I'll try."

Jack and Annie crouched in the grass. They watched and waited as the knights danced closer . . . and closer . . . and closer. . . .

"Now!" shouted Annie.

Jack and Annie rushed forward. They broke into the circle on either side of the knights. As Jack started dancing, his feet seemed to fly to the beat of the drum. He felt a wave of great joy. His worries left him.

"*Now*, Jack!" cried Annie. "Pull away!"

But Jack didn't want to pull away. The music rang in his ears. Nothing mattered except the dancing.

"Jack! Pull away NOW!" Annie shouted again.

Jack shook his head, trying to shake off Annie's voice.

"*Morgan! Morgan!*" Annie yelled.

The word *Morgan* made Jack stumble a bit in the dance.

"*Morgan! Morgan!*" Annie shouted.

Jack stumbled again. Then he used all his might to stop himself from dancing. He let go of the hand of the dancer on his right and threw himself out of the dance—pulling the knight on his left with him. Annie and the other two knights tumbled back with them onto the grass.

Just as before, the dancers didn't seem to notice. They closed their circle and kept going round and round in their joyous, timeless dance.

# CHAPTER TEN

# The Knights' Gifts

The three knights lay in the grass, fighting for breath.

"The dance . . . We must stop . . . stop dancing," gasped the older knight.

"You *have* stopped! We pulled you away!" said Annie.

The knight looked up at her and Jack. He had a rough, craggy face.

"Who . . . who are you?" he asked in a hoarse voice.

"Friends!" said Annie. She spoke loudly to be

heard over the music. "We come from King Arthur's castle!"

"We're on a quest," said Jack, "to get the Water of Memory and Imagination."

"To save Camelot!" said Annie.

"Camelot—" whispered the knight. "We come from Camelot.... I don't recognize you...."

"We're just visiting," said Annie. "But we know all about *you*. You're Sir Lancelot, aren't you?"

"Yes," breathed the knight.

"And Sir Percival and Sir Galahad," said Jack.

"Yes...my son, Galahad...," said the knight.

"King Arthur thinks you are lost forever," said Annie.

Sir Lancelot closed his eyes. "The dance...," he said, "it made us forget...."

"I know," said Jack. "The dancers must be

the Keepers of the Cauldron. You can't get past them without getting caught up in their dance."

"Father . . . we must find . . . the water. . . ." Sir Galahad tried to sit up, but he was too weary. He lay back in the grass.

"That's okay, we're here now," said Annie. "You should all rest."

Sir Galahad closed his eyes.

"Yeah, don't worry," said Jack. "Annie and I will find the magic water for Camelot."

"But you . . . you are just children," said Sir Percival, the third knight. "You must wait . . . for us. . . ."

"There's no time to wait," said Jack.

"Camelot is dying!" said Annie. "We have to hurry!"

"Then you must . . . take this . . . ," said Sir Galahad. He reached into a leather pouch that hung around his shoulder. He took out a silver cup. With a trembling hand, the young knight gave the cup to Annie.

"A cup!" she said.

"Take . . . this, too," said Sir Percival. He pulled a small wooden box from a bag that hung from his belt. He handed it to Jack.

Jack opened the lid. In the middle of the box was a pointer with markings all around it.

"A compass!" said Jack.

"And this . . . ," said Sir Lancelot. He took a silk cord from around his neck. A glass key hung from the cord.

"A key!" whispered Annie.

Lancelot handed the key to Annie. She and Jack looked at it closely. Then Annie hung it around her neck. When she turned back, all the knights were fast asleep.

"Sweet dreams," Annie said gently. "You guys need a long nap."

Jack and Annie stood up.

"I think we have all our gifts now," Jack said. "But I'd better make sure."

He hurried to get his backpack. It was lying in the grass near the knights' swords. He pulled out his notebook and read the second rhyme:

*"Four gifts you will need—*
*The first from me.*
*Then a cup, a compass,*
*And, finally, a key."*

"Great," said Annie. "We got the cloak from the Christmas Knight and the other three gifts from them. This quest is really easy."

Jack shook his head.

"It's not over yet," he said. "We still have to find the cauldron with the Water of Memory and Imagination."

"We'll find it," said Annie. "Read the third rhyme."

Jack looked in his notebook and read the third rhyme aloud:

*"If you survive to complete your quest,*
*The secret door lies to the west."*

"No problem!" said Annie. "We survived the guards and the dance. Now the *compass* can show us how to go west. And the *key* will unlock the secret door. And we'll fill the *cup* with water from the cauldron! See, it's all easy!"

Jack still felt worried. *A little too easy*, he thought.

"What are we waiting for?" said Annie. "Let's go."

Jack looked down at the compass. "Okay . . . ," he said. "The pointer's pointing north. So west must be *that* way." He pointed left, toward a thicket of bushes and small trees.

"Great," said Annie. "Here, carry the cup in your pack."

Jack put his notebook and the silver cup into his pack. Then he and Annie started into the thicket.

They ducked under branches and pushed

past bushes. Thorns scraped their hands. Twigs snapped against their faces.

Jack kept checking the compass. Could they really be searching in the right place? he wondered. What kind of door would they find in a tangled thicket?

"Listen," said Annie. "It's so quiet now."

The thicket had grown eerily silent. No birds called from the bushes. No music could be heard in the distance.

Jack checked the compass once more. "It says we're still going west," he said. "I just hope this thing works."

"It works," Annie said softly. "Look—" Annie was holding back a leafy branch. She pointed to a rocky hillside beyond the thicket. Halfway up the hillside was a ledge.

Between two giant boulders on the ledge was a shining glass door.

# CHAPTER ELEVEN

# The Crystal Cave

"*The secret door!*" whispered Jack.

"Yes!" said Annie.

Jack dropped the compass into his pack. Then he and Annie scrambled through the bushes and climbed up the rocks to the door.

Annie took Sir Lancelot's glass key from around her neck. She slipped the key into the keyhole. She turned the key slowly.

*Clink.*

"Yippee," Annie said softly. She pushed open the door.

Beyond the door was a huge, glittering cave. The floor, walls, and ceiling were made of clear crystal.

Jack and Annie stepped inside. The cave was filled with dancing streams of purple light.

"It's so bright!" whispered Jack. "Where's all the purple light coming from?"

"There," said Annie. She pointed to a crack on the far side of the cave. "Let's look."

They crossed the cave and peered through the crack into a room. Along the brilliant crystal walls of the room were four doorways.

In the far corner of the room was a fire. The fire blazed with leaping purple flames. Over the flames hung a gleaming golden cauldron.

"There it is," whispered Jack.

"Wow," whispered Annie.

"The cauldron with the Water of Memory and Imagination," whispered Jack.

"I know," whispered Annie. "Let's go!"

They squeezed through the crack, then walked toward the gleaming cauldron. Jack reached into his pack and pulled out Sir Galahad's silver cup.

"The cauldron's too high," said Annie. "We can't get to the water."

"Here, take this," said Jack, handing her the cup. "Climb on my back."

He bent over, and Annie climbed on piggy-back. Jack stood up shakily. "Hurry!" he said. "You're heavy."

"I can't reach it," said Annie. "Move closer."

Jack staggered forward a few steps. Stretching as far as she could, Annie reached again. She skimmed water from the top of the bubbling cauldron, filling the silver cup.

"Got it!" she whispered. "Now set me down. Slowly!"

Annie held the cup with both hands. Jack slowly bent his knees and Annie climbed carefully off his back. They stared silently for a moment at the Water of Memory and Imagination in the cup. It was clear and shimmering.

"Now we can save Morgan," said Annie.

Just then Jack smelled something strange—
it was like the smell of rotten seaweed. He
heard weird gurgling sounds behind them.

He and Annie turned around.

A giant, slimy, mud-colored creature crawled
out through one of the doorways. The creature
was long and scaly like a crocodile but much,

MUCH bigger. It had wings that looked as if they'd been spun from a thousand spiderwebs. It had glowing red eyes and long, curled claws.

The creature opened its huge jaws. Strands of drool dripped from its sharp, pointed teeth. The creature hissed and hot blue flame shot from its mouth.

Another monster crawled through a different doorway, quickly followed by a third, and then a fourth.

"Yikes!" said Annie.

"The *real* Keepers of the Cauldron...," whispered Jack.

## CHAPTER TWELVE

## Fire with Fire

The four *real* Keepers of the Cauldron crawled closer to Jack and Annie, hissing and snorting blue fire.

"What do we do now?" whispered Annie.

"I don't know," said Jack. "We're trapped."

"I have an idea," whispered Annie. "Let's drink the water."

"What?" said Jack.

"It's the Water of Memory and Imagination, right?" said Annie. "So maybe if we drink it, we can *imagine* a way to escape!"

"That's crazy," said Jack.

The Keepers crawled closer, snorting more blue flame and filling the air with their rotten stench.

"Okay, okay, let's try it," said Jack.

Annie took a sip from the silver cup, then handed it to Jack. His hands trembled as he held the cup to his lips and took a sip. The water tasted sweet, bitter, and spicy, all at the same time.

Jack gave the cup back to Annie.

"Now imagine we're saved!" she said.

Jack closed his eyes. He tried to imagine being saved. He pictured the four Keepers crawling back through their doorways.

"Okay. Ready to fight?" said Annie.

Jack opened his eyes. "What? Fight?"

Annie set the silver cup on the floor.

"Now!" she said.

Suddenly, Jack felt like he'd been hit by a bolt of lightning. His fears slipped away. He was filled with strength and fury.

Without thinking, he lunged with Annie toward the wood fire under the cauldron. They each grabbed two long, straight branches from

the edge of the fire. They raised them high in the air. The branches blazed with purple fire like flaming swords.

"AAAHHH!" Jack and Annie shouted.

The four Keepers hissed louder than before. Great balls of blue fire exploded from their mouths and nostrils!

Jack and Annie slashed the air with their fiery weapons, jabbing at the Keepers. They fought fire with fire, blue flame with purple flame.

"Back! Back!" they shouted.

With each jab and shout, Jack felt stronger and braver. Waving their burning branches, he and Annie drove the Keepers toward the walls.

The Keepers' blue flames grew weaker and weaker, as if they were running out of fuel. Finally, one by one, each Keeper slunk back into the doorway from which it had come.

When all the Keepers had disappeared, Jack and Annie placed a burning branch in front of each of the four doorways to keep the monsters from coming back out.

Then they brushed off their hands.

"Let's go," Annie said coolly.

Jack nodded.

Annie carefully picked up the silver cup of water from the cauldron. Then she and Jack squeezed through the narrow crack and strode through the bright crystal cave.

They stepped out into the daylight.

The glass key was still in the keyhole.

Jack calmly locked the door behind them. He handed the key to Annie.

Then Jack's knees gave way, and he sank to the ground.

# CHAPTER THIRTEEN

# Your Horses Are Waiting

"I don't believe what just happened," said Jack.

"What part don't you believe?" said Annie, holding the silver cup.

Jack laughed and shook his head.

"I don't believe *any* of it," he said.

Annie laughed, too. "That was cool, huh?"

Jack pushed his glasses into place and stared at her. "Seriously, what just happened in there?" he asked.

"I imagined us fighting the Keepers with

flaming swords," said Annie. "What did you imagine?"

Jack shrugged. "I—I just imagined the Keepers going back in their holes," he said.

"Good," said Annie. "We both got what we imagined."

"Yeah," said Jack, smiling. "But what *you* imagined made a much better story."

A shriek of fury came from inside the cave.

"Yikes!" said Annie.

"Let's get out of here!" said Jack.

He scrambled to his feet, and together they climbed back down over the big rocks to the thicket. Annie moved very carefully to keep from spilling the water in the cup.

When they came to the thicket, Jack pulled out Sir Percival's compass. "If we came *west* to get here, we have to go *east* to get back," he said. "East is *that* way. . . ."

As they started into the wild growth, Jack went first so he could clear the way for Annie.

Without talking, they pushed steadily through the trees and bushes, moving farther and farther from the Keepers' cave.

Finally, they heard music in the distance. They walked closer and closer toward the sound, until they stepped back into the green glade.

The winged dancers were still there, dancing in their magic circle. Jack's heart raced. He wanted to join them again. But he knew that if he did, he would never escape their dance.

"Look!" said Annie. "The knights are awake!"

Sir Lancelot, Sir Galahad, and Sir Percival were standing just beyond the circle of dancers. They were buckling on their swords.

"Hi!" called Annie. "Guess what! We got it!"

The knights walked shakily toward Jack and Annie. They still looked thin and tired, but color had returned to their cheeks.

"We have the Water of Memory and Imagination," said Annie. She held up the silver cup.

The knights smiled.

"Now we just have to get it back to Camelot," said Jack.

"We would like to help you," said Sir Lancelot. "But it seems we have lost our three horses."

"No, you haven't!" said Annie. "Your horses are waiting for you!"

"They're on the other side of the hill," said Jack.

Jack and Annie led the knights over the hill. On their way, Jack picked up the red velvet cloak. When they came to the meadow, they saw the three horses.

The horses neighed and cantered over to the knights. As Sir Lancelot stroked the mane of the black horse, he turned to Jack and Annie.

"You can both ride back to Camelot with me," he said.

"Thanks!" they said.

Jack fastened the red cloak around his neck. Sir Lancelot helped them onto the back of his horse, then climbed on himself.

Annie sat behind Lancelot. She held on to the knight with her right hand. She held the silver cup in her left hand.

"Can you carry the water without spilling it?" Jack asked her, worried.

"I'll try," she said.

Sir Galahad mounted the brown horse, and Sir Percival climbed on the gray horse. Then the three knights started through the pale green meadow.

"Careful, careful," Jack whispered to Annie.

"I got it, I got it," she said.

When they came to the iron gate, the knights drew their swords.

"Open the gate! In the name of King Arthur of Camelot!" Sir Lancelot called. Though he still sounded hoarse, the knight's deep voice carried an amazing strength.

The iron gate slowly swung open. Sir Lancelot urged his horse onward.

The guards watched silently as the knights passed by them and started across the bridge.

The three horses trod in single file over the wooden planks. Again, Jack was amazed by the difference between this world and the Other-world. Here it was dark and freezing and foggy. The red cloak flapped in the bitter wind.

As the horses stepped off the bridge, they each neighed loudly.

"Oh, wow!" whispered Annie.

Standing high on a rock, in a swirl of fog, was the white stag.

## CHAPTER FOURTEEN

# Return

The three knights gazed in wonder at the white stag.

"Here, take this!" Annie said to Jack. She handed him the silver cup. Then she slipped off the back of Lancelot's horse and ran to the stag.

"Thanks for coming for us!" she cried, throwing her arms around his neck.

The three knights looked at Jack.

"That's the white stag," said Jack. "He brought us here."

"Are you wizards?" Sir Percival asked in a hushed voice.

"No, just ordinary kids," said Jack. "But I know *he's* magic. We got here from Camelot in no time at all. I guess he's come to take us back."

"Then you must go with him," said Sir Lancelot. "You will have a much faster journey, I can assure you."

Sir Lancelot held the silver cup as Jack slipped down from the black horse. Then Jack took the cup and carefully climbed onto the back of the stag behind Annie. He held the cup with both hands as the stag stood up.

"Tell King Arthur we will return to Camelot before the first night of the New Year," said Sir Lancelot.

"Farewell, Jack and Annie!" said Sir Galahad.

"Godspeed!" said Sir Percival.

"Same to you!" said Annie.

"Have a safe trip!" said Jack.

The knights solemnly bowed.

The white stag blew out a puff of frosty air. Then he started down the mountainside.

When the stag came to the base of the mountain, he took off again like a white comet. The red cloak billowed around Jack and Annie, keeping them warm and safe.

The stag dashed across the wintry fields. He ran past quiet stables and thatched huts. He ran past flocks of sheep and herds of goats asleep in meadows. He leaped over frozen streams and stone walls and hedgerows.

The stag ran on and on through the starry night, until he brought Jack and Annie back to the dark castle grounds of Camelot.

He walked over the frozen grass of the outer courtyard. He came to a halt near the grove below the tree house. He knelt in the grass, and Jack and Annie climbed off his back.

Miraculously, the silver cup still brimmed with water from the cauldron. Not a drop had spilled out.

"We'd better leave the cloak here," said Jack, "so I don't trip on it."

Jack carefully set the cup on the ground. Annie helped him unbutton the red velvet cloak from around his neck. Then she draped it over the stag's back.

"To keep you warm and safe," she whispered to him. "And thanks for everything."

"Yeah, thanks," said Jack. "Good-bye."

The white stag stared at them with his mysterious amber eyes. He nodded once. Then he turned and headed into the darkness.

Jack picked up the cup. "Come on!" he said. He started walking quickly through the outer courtyard.

"Careful, careful!" said Annie.

"I got it, I got it," said Jack.

They crossed the drawbridge to the inner courtyard of the castle. Then they pushed open the giant arched doors.

The great hall was just as they had left it— dimly lit and freezing cold. King Arthur, Queen Guinevere, the Knights of the Round Table, and Morgan le Fay were all still frozen and silent.

"What do we do now?" said Jack.

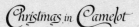

"Let's try putting a drop of water on each of
them! Morgan first!" said Annie.

"Okay," said Jack. "Come on."

Holding his breath and keeping his eyes on
the cup, Jack walked carefully toward the

Round Table. Suddenly, his left foot stepped on the shoelace of his right sneaker—and he stumbled.

"Jack!" yelled Annie.

Jack tried to regain his balance, but it was too late! As he fell to the floor, the silver cup slipped from his hands.

## CHAPTER FIFTEEN

# Christmas Magic

Jack and Annie watched in horror as the water from the cup splashed over the stone floor. It trickled into the cracks between the stones and disappeared.

Jack scrambled to the cup. He picked it up. It was completely empty.

"Oh, no," Jack moaned. He sat back and put his head in his hands. *Camelot will never wake up now*, he thought. *The legend will end forever.*

"Jack!" said Annie. "Look!"

Jack raised his head. He pushed his glasses

into place. A golden cloud was rising from the cracks between all the stones of the floor.

The cloud spread quickly throughout the great hall, filling the room with wonderful smells—the scent of cedar smoke and evergreen, of roses and almonds.

The cloud rose up and up, then wafted out through the upper windows of the hall. Suddenly, a white dove flew through one of the windows. It soared across the dark room like a bright light, then swooped back out into the night.

Soft, gentle laughter came from the end of the hall. The laughter grew louder. Jack saw King Arthur and Queen Guinevere looking at one another—they were laughing! The Knights of the Round Table were laughing, too!

Best of all, Jack saw Morgan le Fay smiling at him and Annie!

"Jack! Annie! Come here!" she called. She held out her arms.

"Morgan!" cried Annie. She ran to Morgan and threw her arms around the enchantress. Jack stood up. Still holding the empty cup, he ran to Morgan and hugged her, too.

"We did what the Christmas Knight told us to do!" said Annie. "We brought back the Water of Memory and Imagination!"

"But I dropped the cup," said Jack, "and spilled all the water!"

"But the water made a gold cloud," said Annie. "And everyone came back to life!"

Morgan laughed with amazement.

"You have just returned from the Other-world?" she asked.

"Yes!" said Annie.

"A white stag brought us back!" said Jack. He turned to King Arthur.

"Your Majesty," he said, "we have good news. Your knights are safe. Sir Lancelot said to tell you they'll be home before the first night of the New Year."

The king looked bewildered. "You found them—?"

"Yes, and they're all fine," said Annie.

"Here—" said Jack. He handed the silver cup to the king. "Please give this back to Sir Galahad."

"And this to Sir Lancelot," said Annie. She took the glass key from around her neck and gave it to King Arthur.

"Oh, and this to Sir Percival," said Jack. He pulled the wooden compass box from his pack and gave it to the king.

At first, King Arthur was too stunned to speak. Then he clapped his hands and laughed joyfully.

"Thank you!" he said to Jack and Annie.

The Knights of the Round Table all cheered.

"Ring the bells!" King Arthur shouted. "Call the people of Camelot to the castle!"

"They have already gathered outside the doors, Your Majesty," said a page.

"Bring them in!" said King Arthur. "We must rejoice together!"

Queen Guinevere smiled at Jack and Annie. Her eyes sparkled now. "Once again, you have helped save Camelot," she said. "Thank you very much."

"You're welcome," said Jack and Annie together.

Then Jack heard the sounds of children talking and laughing. He turned to see a crowd of people streaming through the arched doorway of the great hall. They carried candles, a giant fir tree, and boughs of holly and pine. Musicians followed them with stringed instruments.

As everyone started to decorate the hall, the musicians began playing and singing a beautiful Christmas carol.

"Jack!" said Annie. "Look!"

The white stag was standing in the arched doorway.

Jack turned excitedly to Morgan. "See that

white stag?" he said. "He took us to the Otherworld! See him?"

Morgan smiled.

"Yes, I *do* see him," she said. "And now I see
*everything*."

Jack looked back at the doorway. The stag
was gone. In his place stood an old man with a
long white beard. He held a staff and wore a
flowing red cloak—the same cloak Jack and
Annie had worn on their quest.

"Who's that?" Jack asked.

"That is Merlin the magician," said Morgan. "It was *Merlin* who invited you here. I see that now."

"Merlin?" said Jack. "*He* sent us the Royal Invitation?"

"Yes," said Morgan. "Then he put the rest of us under a spell. And he carried you to the Otherworld."

"No," said Annie, "the *Christmas Knight* put you under a spell."

"And the *white stag* carried us to the Otherworld," said Jack.

Morgan smiled.

"Merlin was both the Christmas Knight and the white stag," she said. "Remember, he's a magician, not a mortal. He can change his shape whenever he wishes."

"Oh, wow," whispered Annie.

"Why did Merlin do these things?" asked Jack.

"Merlin was angry when King Arthur banished magic from Camelot," said Morgan. "I see now he finally took matters into his own hands."

"How?" said Jack.

"He knew King Arthur would send no more knights to the Otherworld for the Water of Memory and Imagination," said Morgan. "So I assume he brought you to Camelot hoping that you would offer to go instead."

"Why did he want *us* to go?" asked Annie.

"Merlin has often heard my tales of your adventures in the tree house," said Morgan. "He knows you both have a great desire to fight for the good. And he knows you use the gift of imagination very well. Those are two special qualities needed to succeed in *any* quest."

Jack and Annie looked back at Merlin. From far across the room, the white-bearded magician smiled at them. He raised his staff. Then he slipped out the door.

Jack looked around the great hall. All the

candles and torches were lit now. A fire blazed in the hearth. The musicians were playing. Everyone was singing. The room glowed with warm firelight and rosy faces.

At last, Christmas in Camelot was just as Jack had imagined it would be. The spell of the Dark Wizard had been broken. The great hall was filled with beauty and love and joy and light.

# CHAPTER SIXTEEN

## Welcome Home

"Wake up, Jack," said Annie.

Jack opened his eyes.

He was lying in the dark on the wooden floor of the tree house. Through the window, he saw the cloudy sky above the Frog Creek woods.

"Time to go home," said Annie.

"Oh, I must have fallen asleep," said Jack. "I had the most incredible dream. I dreamed that we went to Camelot. It was Christmas, and Merlin—"

"That wasn't a dream," said Annie. "It was

real. You fell asleep at the Round Table during the party. King Arthur carried you to the tree house. And I made the wish for us to come home."

Jack sat up.

"Seriously?" he whispered.

"Seriously," she said.

"Ja-ack! An-nie!" their mom called in the distance.

"Coming!" Annie shouted out the tree house window. She turned to Jack. "Let's go!"

"I mean—seriously? It *really* happened?" Jack asked Annie again.

"Yes! Really!" she said. She held up the Royal Invitation. "See? Proof."

"Oh . . . yeah," he whispered.

"This time, the letter *M* stood for Merlin, not Morgan," said Annie.

Jack smiled.

"Thanks, Merlin," he said softly.

Jack picked up his backpack. Then he and

Annie started down the rope ladder and headed home. As they walked through the deep December twilight, snowflakes started to fall.

By the time they left the woods and headed down their street, snow was swirling everywhere. Ahead they could see their house glowing with lamplight. Their mom was waiting on their front porch.

"Hi, Mom!" said Annie.

"Hi, Mom!" said Jack.

"Hi, kids. Did you have a good day?" she asked.

"Yeah," said Jack.

"Pretty good," said Annie.

"I'm glad," said their mom. "Welcome home." She held the door open, and Jack and Annie slipped inside.

Their house felt extra warm and cozy. Good smells came from the kitchen. Jack and Annie took off their snow-covered jackets, then headed up the stairs.

In the hallway, Annie turned to Jack. "Merry Christmas," she said simply.

"Merry Christmas," he said.

Annie slipped into her room, and Jack into his.

Jack closed his door and sat on his bed. He took his notebook out of his pack and opened it. His spirits sank. Except for the three rhymes, he'd taken no notes on their journey—not one.

Exhausted, Jack lay back on his bed. He squeezed his eyes shut. He tried to remember the details of their adventures in Camelot and the Otherworld.

He could feel the terrible chill in the great hall when Morgan was frozen. He could hear the joyful music as the winged dancers danced around in their circle. He could taste the sweet, bitter, spicy taste of the Water of Memory and Imagination.

Jack sat up. All at once, he felt very awake. He turned to a clean page in his notebook. He grabbed his pencil and wrote:

It all started when we saw the white
dove in the twilight. . . .

Using his memory and his imagination, Jack
kept writing, doing his part to keep the legend
of King Arthur, the Knights of the Round Table,
Merlin, and Morgan le Fay alive.

As the snow swirled outside his window, Jack
wrote and wrote and wrote. He didn't stop
writing until he had written down the whole
story—*his* story of their Christmas in Camelot.

# A Note from the Author

Many people believe that the legend of King Arthur was inspired by an actual military leader who led Britain over 1,500 years ago.

Imaginary stories about the adventures of King Arthur were first told in Wales and Ireland. These stories are called Celtic myths. Sadly, most Celtic myths are lost to us forever because only a few were written down. Many details in my story about King Arthur's realm are drawn from details in the few Celtic stories that have survived through the ages.

The **cloak** that makes one invisible was

considered to be one of "the Thirteen Treasures of Britain." Merlin the magician was said to keep the treasures in a glass tower. None of the magic of the treasures would work for a person who was unworthy to use them.

The **white stag** was inspired by a supernatural Celtic beast that often led humans to a hidden Otherworld.

The idea for the **Cauldron of Memory and Imagination** came from a 6th-century poem. The poem tells a story about King Arthur and his knights traveling to a hidden world and searching for a magical cauldron of poetry and inspiration. Many knights never returned from that dangerous quest.

In the 12th century, Queen Eleanor of Aquitaine encouraged poets and troubadours to make up more stories about King Arthur and the Knights of the Round Table to inspire her people. In the following years, storytellers all over Europe told heroic tales of King Arthur,

Merlin, Sir Lancelot, Queen Guinevere, and Morgan le Fay. French poets were the first to call the imaginary kingdom *Camelot*.

The storytellers of the Middle Ages blended elements of Christianity with the old Celtic myths. In their stories, miracles and marvels often took place around Christian holidays. **Christmas in Camelot** was a time of joyous celebration.

*Mary Pope Osborne*

# Fun Activities for Jack and Annie and *You!*

## Christmas Craftwork!

It can be hard to wait for your favorite holiday. Many families buy a special type of calendar, called an Advent calendar, to help them count down the days until Christmas. But you can make your own Advent calendar to celebrate the season and count down to December 25.

And if you're *extra* creative, you can make this activity work for any holiday you love—whether it's Hanukkah, Halloween, or your own birthday! Think about what shapes and colors work best for different celebrations, and let your imagination run wild.

### Advent Calendar
You will need:
- A large piece of green poster board
- Twenty-four small squares of Velcro
- Colored construction paper
- Glue
- Pens, markers, or crayons
- Scissors (with adult supervision)

1. Draw a large Christmas tree on your piece of green poster board. Ask an adult to help you cut out the tree along the lines that you've drawn. Make sure the tree is big enough for all the decorations you will create!

2. Take your twenty-four squares of Velcro and pull them apart. Now you have twenty-four sharp sides and twenty-four soft sides.

3. Glue the twenty-four sharp pieces of Velcro onto your Christmas tree. Be sure to space them out, and put one piece at the very top of your tree.

4. Use construction paper to create twenty-four ornaments for your tree. Your ornaments can be circles, like the familiar Christmas bulbs used by many families. Or you can try more complex shapes like bells, hearts, and candy canes.

5. Use pens, markers, or crayons to decorate your ornaments, but leave a blank space in the center of each one. You will need the blank space when you give each ornament a number.

6. With a marker, write a number on each of your ornaments, from one to twenty-four. The ornament that will go on the top of the tree should be

number one. It is usually a star, but it can be whatever you want.

7. With glue, attach the twenty-four soft pieces of Velcro to the backs of your twenty-four ornaments.

8. Starting December 1, place one ornament on your tree each day, beginning with number twenty-four. This tells you there are twenty-four days until Christmas! On Christmas Eve, you'll place ornament number one on the top of your tree.

9. After Christmas, you can store your calendar in a safe place. Next year, remove your ornaments and use the Advent calendar all over again.

# Puzzle of Memory and Imagination

Jack and Annie learned many new things on their adventure in Camelot. Did you?

Put your knowledge to the test with this puzzle. You can use a notebook or make a copy of this page if you don't want to write in your book.

1. The name of King Arthur's kingdom.

☐ ☐ ☐ ☐ ◯ ☐ ☐

2. The name of King Arthur's queen.

◯ ☐ ☐ ☐ ☐ ☐ ☐ ☐ ☐

3. The shape of the table where King Arthur and his knights sit.

☐ ☐ ☐ ◯ ☐

4. The most famous of Camelot's knights.

☐ ☐ ☐

☐ ☐ ☐ ☐ ◯ ☐ ☐ ☐

## 5. The enchanted land where Morgan says magic began.

☐ ☐ ☐ ☐ ☐ ☐ ☐ ☐ ☐ ◯

## 6. The white-bearded magician of Camelot.

☐ ◯ ☐ ☐ ☐ ☐

Now look at your answers above. The letters that are circled spell a word—but that word is scrambled! Can you unscramble it to spell the name of a certain kind of story? Here's a hint: This type of story begins with a bit of truth, but is changed by the imaginations of different people in different times.